THE WHISTLE-BELL TRAIN

by
LEE RYLAND

illustrated by
FRANK ALOISE

WHITMAN PUBLISHING
DIVISION
Western Publishing Company, Inc.
Racine, Wisconsin

Produced in the U.S.A.

EAT AT
JONES'
FRESH GROCERIES
BLACKBERRY STATION

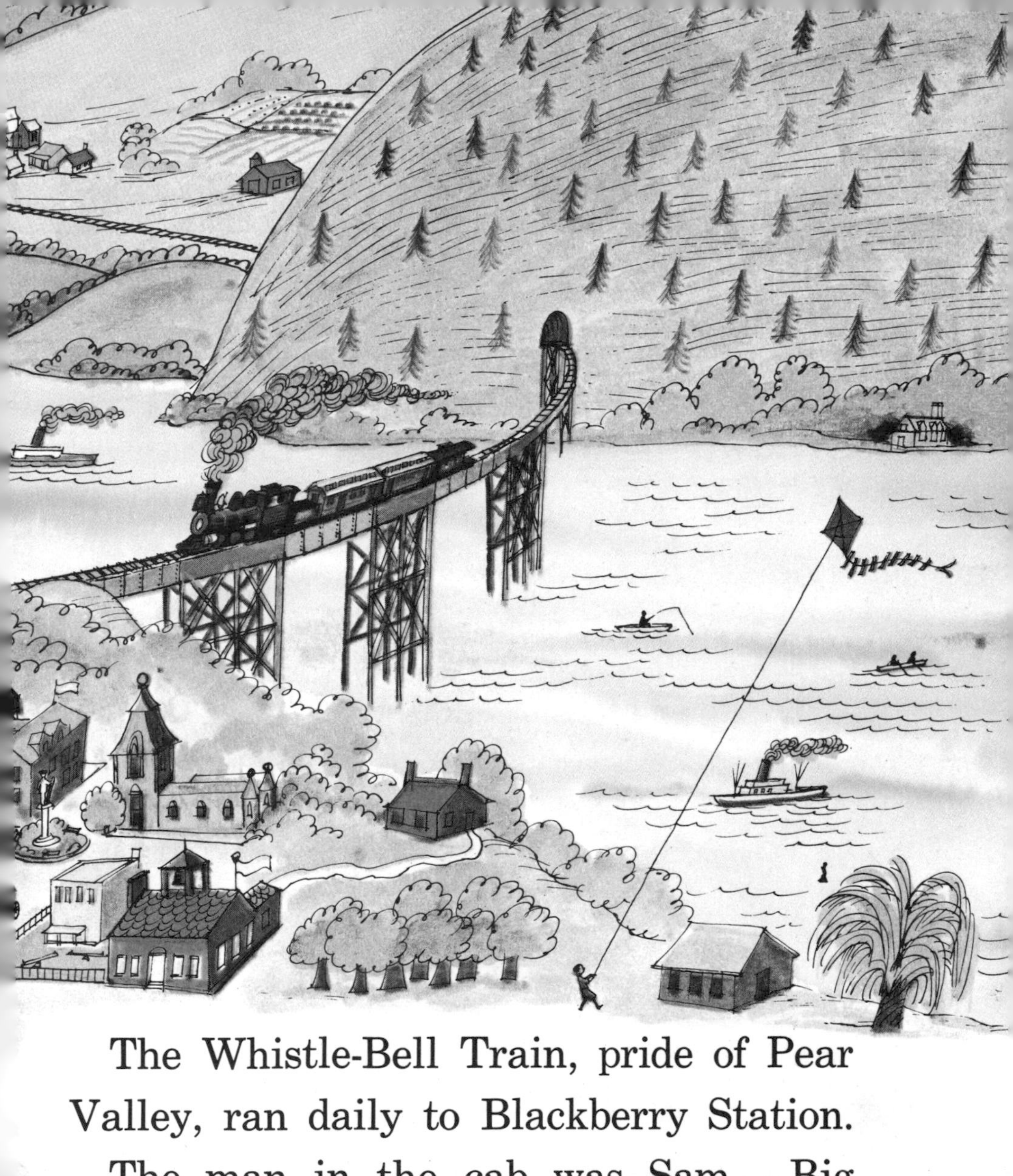

The Whistle-Bell Train, pride of Pear Valley, ran daily to Blackberry Station.

The man in the cab was Sam — Big Sam.

One fine spring day, Big Sam got ready to roll. He looked out from the Whistle-Bell Train. "What's *that* up on top of my red caboose?" he wondered. "It's a red, red robin — I *think*. And it's hopping and chirping and cheeping.

"Shoo! Fly away!" called Big Sam. "Robins don't ride on trains. Hardly ever!"

It's a long, long way to Blackberry Station. Big Sam took the Whistle-Bell Train through a dark tunnel.

Big Sam took the Whistle-Bell Train *clickety-clack, clickety-clack* over a tall railroad bridge.

Big Sam came to a curve. He looked out from the Whistle-Bell Train at the cars behind. "What's *that* up on top of my red caboose?" he wondered. "It's a red, red robin — I'm *sure*. And it's *still* hopping and chirping and cheeping!"

Right on time, twelve o'clock noon, the Whistle-Bell Train rolled into Blackberry Station. *Now* where was the red, red robin? Big Sam ran back to his caboose to find out.

The Ticket Taker (who is boss of the tickets) ran. The Stationmaster (who is boss of the station) ran. They wanted to see why Big Sam was running.

The red, red robin saw them coming.

She flew under the steps of the red caboose.

Frightened little robin.

The Stationmaster took out his Rule Book. He asked, "Big Sam, was *that* robin riding on your red caboose?"

The Ticket Taker opened his Ticket Book. He said, "*No one* rides free. No one. Not even *me*!"

Big Sam answered, "What *I* want to know is this: *Why* is *that* robin *under* my caboose?"

And Big Sam peeked at the robin to find out.

"What do you see?" asked the Stationmaster, who was watching.

"What do you think?" asked the Ticket Taker, who was wondering.

Big Sam smiled. "I *see* Mrs. Red, Red Robin on a nest. I *think* she has one, two, three blue-green eggs under her."

Is that right, Mrs. Robin?

The Stationmaster sat in his office. He read in the Rule Book. He said, "You *can not* stop the Whistle-Bell Train for a robin. You've got to go, Big Sam. Go!"

The Ticket Taker looked in his Ticket Book. He said, "Mrs. Robin can't go! She has no ticket. And no one rides free on *this* train. Not ever!"

But, how much is a ticket for a red, red robin and three blue-green eggs?

What did Big Sam do about this? He put the red caboose — *crash-bang* — on a siding.

Was Mrs. Robin afraid? She was not!

Did Mrs. Robin leave her nest of three blue-green eggs? She did not!

Faithful Mrs. Robin.

Then Big Sam found a can of paint, a brush, and a board. He painted a sign.

Big Sam hung his sign on the red caboose. He said, very firmly, "Don't let *anyone* move this caboose. It belongs to Mrs. Robin — for now."

The Station-
master shook
his Rule Book
at Big Sam.
He said, "You
can not leave
without the
red caboose!"

The Ticket
Taker walked
about, waving
his Ticket
Book. He
said, "It *just*
isn't done.
Even *with*
a ticket!"

Did you hear
that, Mrs. Robin?

Big Sam looked down from his cab. He said, "I'm sorry, but the Whistle-Bell Train wouldn't be the pride of Pear Valley if I didn't take care of everyone on it. Even robins!"

Every day Mrs. Red, Red Robin sat, cozy and quiet, on her nest of three blue-green eggs.

Every day Big Sam made his long run from Pear Valley. And he always left part of his lunch for — you know who.

Hungry Mrs. Robin.

Every day the Ticket Taker peeked under the red caboose. "No ticket," he sighed. "It *can't* be!" And he looked in his book for a ticket marked "Robins."

Every day the Stationmaster watched the Whistle-Bell Train roll in. "No caboose," he grumbled. "It just is *not* right!" And he looked again in his Rule Book under "cabooses."

On the first day of May, Mrs. Robin and her three little robins were hopping and chirping and cheeping.

"Howdy," said Big Sam. "If you don't need my caboose, I can hitch up and head back to Pear Valley."

What do you say, Mrs. Robin? Chirrup-chirrup! Thank you! Thank you!

The Stationmaster stopped by. He said, "Big Sam, you did a fine job on the Whistle-Bell Train. But I hope the *use* of the red caboose won't become a *habit*—for robins!"

The Ticket Taker called, "Mrs. Robin, I'd like to say: You *didn't* need a ticket. I can see you raised your babies *without* one!"

Good-bye, Mrs. Robin. Good-bye.
So long, Big Sam. So long.